WARNING

This book contains sexually explicit scenes and adult language. It may be considered offensive to some readers. This book is for sale to adults ONLY.

* * * * * * * * * * * * * * * * * * *

Please store your files wisely where they cannot be accessed by underage readers.

Other Books by Darla Dunbar:

<u>The Romeo Alpha BBW Paranormal Shifter Romance Series</u>

Amanda Walker thinks that she has a normal and boring life. That is until after her 24th birthday. Everything changes when she meets the man who says he was supposed to be her husband. Denying everything the man says, she fights him every step of the way. But after he kidnaps her, Amanda discovers that there are some things about her family that her parents kept a secret all these years. Among the history of the family she learns secrets she thought only happened in story books. Can Amanda tell the difference between truth and lies or is she this mysterious woman that holds the key to a legacy?

<u>Romeo Alpha Blood Lines Romance Series</u>

Twenty-four years have passed in relative peace for Amanda and Romeo. They've raised five children into adulthood and are thoroughly enjoying their lives as the Alpha King and Queen of the werewolves. At twenty-four, Sarina is just stepping into her powers and will be ripe for mating when her birthday comes in two weeks. What no one knows is the danger that lurks just outside their tight knit community. Romeo has made peace with the other clans and has enjoyed that peace, but it will all come crashing down around him when his oldest daughter comes of age to take a mate.

The Alpha Feud BBW Paranormal Shifter Romance Series

Eliza's life consisted of reporting on boring, crowd-pleasing events, like their country livestock fair. With the arrival of two handsome brothers, the lives of Eliza and her best friend, Melissa, are shaken to the core. For Eliza, the arrival of this new man becomes a test of her relationship with her current boyfriend, who she's been happily living with for over six years. Does Hayden, a complete stranger, really wield the power to make Eliza reconsider her relationship with Andrew?

The Alpha Packed BBW Paranormal Shifter Romance Series

Darlene has led a quiet life since suffering through a terrible break-up. She wants nothing more than to spend her time in front of the TV, away from any sort of trouble. But all that goes down the drain when handsome, rugged and rough Idris comes into her life. He is a werewolf on the lookout for his missing pack leader. Darlene quickly finds herself pulled towards this mysterious man and at the same time finds herself falling deeper and deeper into the world of the supernatural.

The Mind Talker Paranormal Romance Series

Ananda finds herself on the run and she's not alone. With help from Jared, a stranger that she just met, the two evade capture by an organization that is intent on hunting her kind. Ananda and Jared are able to read minds. When an unfortunate incident happened involving a disturbed individual that resulted in the death of his schoolmates, the secret organization decided to take action.

<u>The Leather Satchel Paranormal Romance Series</u>

Valtina is stuck in Middle World, unable to pass on to The Afterlife. In order to redeem herself from past deeds done, she must help bring romance back into the world and stop The Dark Side from destroying love in its entirety. Following orders issued by Ladaya and armed with a leather satchel filled with the appropriate tools and weapons, Valtina embraces each mission with enthusiasm.

Get the latest update on new releases from the author at:

https://darladunbar.com/newsletter/

This book is Part Nine of "<u>The Daemon Paranormal Romance Chronicles</u>"

Book 1 - The Awakening

Phoebe grew up not knowing her mother. The stranger, Apollo Mikos, claimed to know her mother. After that day, Phoebe's life would change forever.

Book 2 - The Shifter

Phoebe is surprised when her dog, Ace, shows up from nowhere. She is on a mission with Apollo to kill the Qilin. That is the only way that the true leader of daemons will emerge.

Book 3 - Forgotten

Juno has been stirring up trouble that has prolonged the infighting among the daemons. In order to get her to stop, Phoebe agrees to give up a year of her memories. But making deals with a siren is never a good thing. Without her memories, Phoebe's romantic relationship with Supay no longer exists. Instead, she leaves Supay for Apollo.

Book 4 - The Siren's Trap

The unsuspecting couple, Phoebe and Supay, made a deal with Juno to stop the infighting among the daemons. But at what price? An entire year was wiped clean from Phoebe's mind. Now Phoebe was with Apollo. Desperate to get her back, Supay considers Juno's new deal. Is it worth the price to pay for the dubious result? To win back Phoebe's love, Supay will need to be unfaithful to her.

Book 5 - Exposed

Hiding away in Peru, Supay and Phoebe start their own family, away from the chaos and the daemon infighting. Meanwhile, Apollo, heart-broken and lost, is lured into another one of Juno's schemes. Making deals with a siren never turns out right. If Apollo accepts the deal, the love of his life may resent him for the rest of his natural life. If he doesn't take the deal, she is lost to him forever.

Book 6 - The Beginning

As preparations for the war between daemons are underway, everyone must begin to choose. Siding temporarily with Apollo, Juno has a moment to look back on her life and figure out how she arrived at this moment. As she sifts through memories of the past, a specific dark stranger stands out. How far will young Juno go with her new love? More importantly, will her mother, Circe, discover the secret tryst?

Book 7 - The Treachery

Having broken the cardinal rule of the sirens, Juno must take action to save her own life and the life of her unborn child. In order to keep her secret safe from the sisterhood, she must kill her lover and conceal her shame. Will Juno betray the sisterhood and save her lover or will she remain loyal by slaying him instead?

Book 8 - Duplicity

Juno's mother, Circe, discovers her lies and gives her an ultimatum to fix everything. As Juno races against the clock to protect her loved ones from Circe, she makes a final choice that could leave her perpetually unhappy. Left to wander the world alone, Juno realizes that freedom means nothing if there is no one to share it with. The nature of Juno's vendetta—and the means she achieves it with—are finally revealed.

Book 9 - Reconnaissance

As Juno's hunt for the daemon's fortress unfolds, Apollo is left alone wondering if she will truly return to him. Will Juno be able to resist her base instincts? More importantly, will she be able to get to the fortress and return without being spotted? Discover how Juno's stealth mission works out.

Book 10 - The Interrogation

Juno tries to hide her rising fear in the presence of her captors. As her fear mounts, she holds on to the hope that Phoebe or Supay will take pity on her. Before that can happen, she has to come clean to Supay about her past. Could he possibly forgive her for what she has done? Will Juno remain faithful to Apollo or will her siren urges take over? Discover how the confrontation with Supay unfolds.

The Daemon Paranormal Romance Chronicles

Reconnaissance

Book Nine

By Darla Dunbar

Copyright Revelry Publishing 2015

Table of Contents

Chapter One

WAKING UP early in the morning, Juno gazed around the room. The cold walls of the castle stood in stark contrast to Apollo's blonde hair. Wearily rubbing her eyes, Juno rolled over and started to get out of bed. Next to her, Apollo struggled sleepily to pull her closer. Juno smiled and stepped away from the bed.

Putting on a robe, she waved her hand across the surface of the scrying basin. After revisiting the memories of her past, she had tried to see across time to the present. She needed to know what Phoebe, Supay and the Greek daemons were preparing to do. Despite her many attempts at scrying across the oceans, she could not get the present to reveal itself to her. The only reasonable answer was that the Greek daemons had chosen to block their activities from prying eyes, but Juno hoped that this was not the case. If she was not able to scry, she would have to go straight to the source to gather intelligence on the opposing side's forces.

Gazing into the ebony basin, few images appeared on the surface of the water. Shifting her gaze slightly, Juno switched between images of the Roman preparations to families cooking breakfast. Nothing appeared in the basin that seemed even remotely connected to the Greeks.

Leaning back heavily, Juno sighed. Her only task with the Romans was to gather intelligence. She had made a deal with Supay and Phoebe that she would not actively participate in the daemon war or stir up trouble. This was the only thing that she could do to stay involved. Glancing over at Apollo, Juno sighed again. This was also the only way for her to stay near Apollo.

Wandering over to the window, Juno looked out over the preparations. The many archers positioned along the wall were unnerving enough. Last night, she had been told that an offensive plan was being readied. Although the Roman daemons wanted to keep the fighting quiet on the island of Sicily, they had no compunctions about drawing attention in Crete. Here, they would use archers, boiling tar and daggers to defend the castle. Over on the island of Crete, they were willing to use any manner of mortar, machine gun, mine or pistol. It was not looking good for Supay and Phoebe. Juno snorted. Not that she cared about Phoebe, but it would be heart wrenching to see anything happen to Supay.

A sound behind her indicated that Apollo was starting to wake up. Running her hands through her hair, Juno approached the bed. Slowly opening his eyes, Apollo caught sight of Juno and smiled. "There's my lovely lady," he murmured as he pulled her in for a kiss. Over the last few weeks, Apollo and Juno had grown increasingly close. What started as a simple, physical fling had transformed into something more. As of yet, Juno was not entirely sure how she felt. After her youthful romance with Supay years ago, she had forsworn any type of love or romantic entanglements.

In reality, she had almost militantly stuck to the siren's code to never fall in love and only have sex for enjoyment or manipulation. During the last few weeks, she had enjoyed the closeness of her relationship with Apollo and the blossoming friendship.

Smiling gently down at Apollo, Juno ran her lips along the outline of his neck. She playfully bit his ear before rumpling his tousled hair. Opening his eyes fully, Apollo grinned and grabbed her by the hips. Rolling over, he positioned her beneath him. He pushed his body against hers so that she could feel how hard he was. "You're not the only one who can tease, my dear siren."

Grinning wickedly, Juno shifted her hips up to his. Her delicate folds moistened the tip of his cock and gave him a taste of what would follow. Moaning, Apollo resisted the urge to enter her. Rocking her hips away from him, Juno kissed Apollo again. "If it were a competition involving teasing, I think that you would lose," she said mockingly.

Raising his eyebrow, Apollo looked ready to contradict her statement. He thought better of starting a useless argument and glanced down at her body instead. In the early morning light, her breasts cast soft shadows along her breastbone. Pushing the sides of her robe apart, he leaned down and took her nipple in his mouth. Flicking his tongue in circles, he teased the tip of her nipple until the rosy, sensual buds became hard, tight circles. Heaving a sigh of satisfaction, Apollo entered her in one slow, fluid motion.

With a tenderness that was out of character for Apollo, he gently made love to Juno as the dawn transformed into daylight. Together, they merged their hips over and over again in a hypnotic fashion. Juno gazed into Apollo's eyes without looking away and what she saw surprised her. The feelings that were developing for Apollo were reciprocated. Shocked, Juno realized that she was no longer just an attractive fling for Apollo. Somehow, they had transformed into something more. What they were at the moment did not have a name or a label. Their fledgling relationship existed in a delicate balance that should not be harmed with such a crass thing as a label.

Moaning softly, Juno pushed her hips against Apollo's body. Despite her enjoyment of their lovemaking, she was losing control. She could not wait through the tenderness and care of making love. Instead, she needed him. Barely able to control her desire, Juno tightened around his cock. The sudden pressure caused an instant wave of pleasure to pass through Apollo's body. Responding to her increased pace, Apollo began to thrust deeper and deeper inside of Juno. Frantically, they moved their hips in a rhythm that defied the laws of physics. Grabbing her hips with his hands, Apollo physically pulled her body onto his. The added weight made it impossible for him to slow down. As she moved her hips above his body, Apollo leaned back his head and let out a moan. Above him, Juno started to cry out from the sweet agony of orgasm. Shivering in pleasure, the couple came together before falling back on the bed.

Minutes passed in silence as Apollo and Juno recovered. Juno lay with her head on his shoulder as her fingers gently traced circles along his muscular chest. As their breathing started to slow down to a normal pace, Juno looked up at Apollo. He was not going to like what she was about to tell him.

"Apollo?" she asked. "I need to talk to you about something important."

Pulling her closer, Apollo waited for her to speak. When she did not, he looked down with concern. "What is it, Juno?" he queried.

Juno sat up and picked up the brush on the night table. Slowly, she began brushing the tangles out of her long, raven black hair. Turning back to him, she sighed and set the brush down. "I need to leave here. Not forever, just for a few weeks." She waited for his response.

Confused, Apollo sat up. "Did I do something? What are you leaving for?"

"No, it is nothing like that. I need to leave to gather intelligence on what the Greeks are doing. Every day, I have tried scrying and watching their activities. Despite my best efforts, I have not been able to see one glimpse of what the other side is up to. If we are going to stand even a remote chance of coming out of this on top, we will need that information."

Rubbing his temples, Apollo leaned forward on his knees and thought. He did not like the idea of her traveling to the area where the enemy was located and trying to play at being a spy. It was not safe for her. He sighed again. "Do you really want to do this, Juno?" Apollo glanced at the door and lowered his voice. "You know, both of us had reasons for being here a couple of months ago that don't even exist anymore. Not really, anyhow. Why risk your life for information when you can stay here with me?"

Juno tilted her head to the side as she thought about it. Apollo had originally joined the Romans after losing Phoebe to Supay. Filled with rage, he had wanted to see the woman who scorned him taken down and had willingly joined the Roman side. Juno had joined out of a desire to wreak havoc and continue her meddling like a good siren would do. As Apollo and Juno had developed romantic feelings for each other, both of their reasons had started to fall away gradually. At the moment, Juno was primarily on the Roman side because she was already there. She did not have to ask, but she knew it was the same for Apollo. She shook her head. "If we are here, we have to be fulfilling our tasks. The only thing that I am able to do in this fight is gather information. If I do not do that, they will doubt my loyalties and we both know that that would end badly. As a siren, my faithfulness is already in question." She patted his cheek tenderly. "We really cannot give them any more reasons to question how committed you and I are to this cause."

Apollo held the tips of her fingers in his mouth. He kissed each one individually before looking up at her again. "Are you sure this is what you want to do?" She nodded. Apollo hesitated before beginning to speak again. "You will come back, right?" He was genuinely concerned that she would be gone forever. Although he was starting to care for her, he knew that her instincts would make wandering and random sex more likely than staying with him for a committed relationship.

Juno chuckled kindly and embraced him lovingly. "I will come back. If everything goes well, you should see me in just a week or so. Don't forget me."

Shaking his head, Apollo kissed her as he stood up to get dressed. "That would never happen."

Chapter Two

It had not taken terribly long for Juno to pack her bag. She had chosen to travel light since she had no clue what would await her on the island of Crete. In her pack, she had simply placed binoculars and throwing knives. There was no reason for her to bring a change of clothes because it would only slow her down. She could buy different clothes on the way there and throw out each old outfit. It might be wasteful, but it would allow her to move quickly.

Pulling out the binoculars, Juno gazed toward the open ocean. At the moment, she was impatiently waiting on Gavdos Island. After consulting a map of the island, she had done her best to guess where the Greek daemons were building a fortress. If it were her choice, she would place the fortress within the White Mountains Protected Forest Reserve. This area contained the highest mountains on the island which would make surveillance easier for the Greeks. Likewise, the secluded forest would make preparations easier. If it were her, this would certainly be the spot she would pick.

Unfortunately, figuring out the exact location and getting there would be her main problems. Considering her recognizable figure and seductive voice, it would be impossible for her to just land in Crete and hope that no one would be alerted to her presence. Even on Gavdos Island, she was risking her safety greatly. She was only 45 kilometers off of the coast of Greece and ought to be hiding her face. Instead, she was deliberately courting danger by hiring a local to ferry her to Greece. Since it was no longer tourist season, convincing one of the thirty-five year-round island dwellers to ferry her was a difficult prospect. Finally, the lure of a few thousand euros had convinced one man to take her a kilometer or two offshore and drop her off.

Juno waited impatiently for the ferryman to arrive. In front of her sat one of the dingiest, most decrepit boats that she had ever seen. She wrinkled her nose. If this little dinghy took her safely across the water, she would be surprised. Behind her, she heard a noise. Without pausing to think, she turned on her heel and pulled a throwing dagger from her belt. She had just enough time to adjust her aim away from the man before she released the knife. Whizzing through the air, the dagger sank into the sand a few feet away from the ferryman. Gazing at the knife, he whistled slowly. With effort, Juno managed to smile and apologize.

Not wanting to say another word to this femme fatale, the ferryman slowly began to push his boat from the sand and into the water. Juno wiped the sand off her knife and watched him move. Covered in dirt, the man's clothes were mostly patches that barely held together. *No wonder he accepted my money for such a strange trip... he is completely down on his luck.*

Silently, she got into the boat as the man began to speed away from the shore. Like they agreed, he switched to oars when they were within five kilometers of Crete. Struggling to keep the oars from splashing, he pulled them closer and closer to shore. Since it was nighttime, Juno hoped the approach would go unnoticed. With the naked eye, she could barely make out the shoreline. In a whisper, the man assured her that they were only two kilometers off of the shore. Nodding her assent, Juno handed him the remaining euros. Taking a deep breath, she slipped off the side of the boat and into the water.

As she began to slowly swim toward the shoreline, the lone boat started to paddle back to Gavdos Island in the same way it had left. The cold ocean water was refreshing after Juno's long day and woke her up quickly. Each wave at her back pushed her closer and closer to shore. Even though it was close to six in the morning, there was still no sign of dawn. Beneath the stars, the air was already starting to warm up. In front of her, the rugged shoreline and a few small buildings came into view. If she was lucky, Juno would reach shore before dawn and be able to walk by these few buildings unnoticed.

Little by little, the rocky pebbles of the beach were felt underneath her feet. Afraid of alerting anyone to her presence, Juno sculled gently through the water until it was impossible to move any farther by swimming. Peering to either side, she adopted a crouching position and slowly crept toward the tree line. Once she was safely in the trees, she looked back. Everything was as still as it was before she arrived. After walking several hundred meters into the forest, she stopped and leaned against a tree. Now that she was safe, it was time to consider breakfast and using the map. Pulling out a loaf of bread and cheese, she leaned against a rock and began to eat. With the sun starting to break on the skyline, she pulled out the map to look for possible locations for the Greek daemons. If she followed the long hike through the Samaria gorge, she might be able to find a path on one of the sides. As one of the main hikes for tourists in the area, it would be the easiest path for her to follow and the best way to remain inconspicuous. For these very reasons, it was also likely that a path to the daemon's fort would lie somewhere along the same path. Rolling up her map, she began to set out confidently in the direction of the gorge. Crisscrossing over dry river beds, she inhaled the sweet scent of pine trees as she hiked. Lone hikers dotted the area, but she could tell instantly that they were not daemons. Instead, they were alone like she was, and hiking in the cooler hours of the morning.

Over the next few hours, Juno managed to hike up nearly one thousand meters in elevation. Despite her continued explorations on surrounding paths, she could not manage to find a way to reach the daemon's fort. Sighing in frustration, she changed her goal. Soon, the area would be flooded with tourists who would all want to hike along the scenic gorge. Although she felt comfortable at the moment, each additional hiker increased the chances that she would be spotted.

From the gorge, she spotted a stand of pine trees above her. Climbing up the sloped cliff face, she managed to finally reach the trees. After a long night of swimming and boating, her morning hike had taken all of the remaining energy out of her body. Until the tourists thinned out around evening time, she would stay in her secret hiding spot and catch up on some well-deserved sleep.

Chapter Three

Darkness had long since fallen by the time Juno woke up. Cursing herself for oversleeping, she stopped moving when the sound of footsteps drew nearer. Pulling herself along her stomach, she army crawled as close as she could to the hiking trail. Below her, a trail of five daemons was walking along the pathway. Each carried several bags filled with food. Around their necks, they each wore a Unakite medallion. Juno frowned. No wonder she was unable to watch their preparations. In addition to protecting the wearer from the effects of computers, radiation and radio waves, Unakite also prevented any mind reading or psychic activity. Her scrying would never have been able to catch their preparations.

Army crawling quietly back to her sleeping spot, Juno tossed her food back into the bag and prepared to leave. Following the daemons may be dangerous, but it was the easiest way to find out where their home base was located.

After ensuring that no other daemons were coming along the trail, Juno tiptoed down the face of the cliff until she was back in the gorge. She glanced behind her and above her. This was the worst possible position to be in. Anyone above would easily be able to see her. Likewise, she would be at the mercy of anyone in front or behind her that managed to figure out that she was there. She winced. This plan was going less easily than she had expected. Climbing up the surface of the gorge, she began to walk along the top of the cliff side. It might be more difficult to make her own path up here, but it would limit the amount of risk she faced.

As the hours of the night wore on, Juno wearily stepped between pebbles and rocks on the cliff's edge. Only wind and occasional loose rocks were heard in the silent air of the nighttime. Around her, the barren, rocky landscape was unforgiving. A single misstep could send her plunging into the gorge at her feet or send a pebble downward to alert the daemons of her presence. Thankfully, Juno was in excellent physical shape and oversleeping had helped improve her attention span.

With the difficulty of creating her own trail, she lacked the time necessary to stop and look at her map. By her own judgment, she guessed that they had nearly reached the end of the trail. The base of the Pagnes would be looming before her soon and a terrible climb would begin at that point. For anyone who was not a shepherd and accustomed to the precarious heights, Pagnes would be a dangerous thing to climb at night.

As the daemons in front of her reached Pagnes, Juno breathed a sigh of relief. They were not climbing it after all. Amid the rocky crags, the daemons disappeared one by one behind a rock. It appeared to be some type of small cave opening. Ingenious. Between the Unakite necklaces and an underground environment, it was unsurprising that she had never been able to pick up on the daemons' location.

Shifting onto her haunches, Juno waited patiently to see if any of the daemons would return. As close as she was now, it would be unwise to risk discovery. The most difficult part would be to enter the cave. Presumably, the underground fortress would have more space and hiding spaces for her to slip among.

After reassuring herself that no more daemons were going to exit, Juno climbed down the face of the cliff and slid slowly along the gorge wall. It did not look like there were any daemons on watch. She chuckled silently. Of course, there would not be any guards. Who would bother guarding an entrance that only accepted one person? Really, she was fighting on the wrong side of this battle. Where the Romans had idiotically constructed their castle and battle strategies, the Greeks had created an unbeatable fortress that did not even require guards to stand watch. Although this would be terrible for the coming daemon war, it fortunately meant that a single daemon like her would be able to sneak into the fortress—at least she hoped so.

Chapter Four

After waiting for a cloud to cover the crescent moon, Juno stalked silently like a panther toward the entrance of the cave. Reaching the large rock, she stared at it for a moment in confusion. Moving around to the back, she could not see any space between the rock and the opening that she knew must be here. Frowning, she tried to nudge the rock. Nothing happened. Juno groaned silently to herself. How was she ever supposed to get in?

In the distance, she heard footsteps. Glancing around, she noticed two fairly large rocks nearby. Although they would not be enough to cover her during the day, the rocks should be fine for a nighttime hiding spot. Slipping behind the rocks, she peered out as a lone daemon approached the entrance. Smiling merrily, the muscle-bound daemon began to reach for the rock. With a start, Juno realized the answer. No one else could open the rock. Instead, each group that left the dwelling was bringing a daemon who possessed Herculean or Nemean lion-like strength. Juno closed her eyes. If she was going to get in, this was her only hope.

Silently, she reached for a dagger in her belt. Pulling it up, she flicked her wrist effortlessly. The dagger soared through the air until it lodged in the man's stomach. Groaning, he looked around for the source of the dagger. His eyes quickly found Juno hidden among the shadows.

Stepping away from the rocks, Juno pulled another dagger from her belt. "Open the rock entrance and let me in. If you do as I say, I will not throw the remaining daggers at your throat."

The man looked Juno up and down speculatively. If he recognized her, he did not give any signs of it. Nodding his assent, the man reached for the rock and pushed it aside. Holding the dagger in front of her, Juno began to walk into the entrance. Before she could enter the cave, the man dropped the rock and reached for her body. Instantly, Juno threw the dagger into his throat and started to run. Before she could leave, the man swept her up like a rag doll over his shoulder. Juno reached for another dagger and the man began laughing.

"Sorry about that. You're Juno, aren't you?" He chuckled merrily as he swept the door open with his other arm. Despite Juno's wriggling, she was unable to escape from his strong hold. Entering a passageway, the man let the rock fall back over the opening with a thud. As the door closed, the man stretched his stomach and the dagger fell out of it. Juno's eye's widened as the knife clattered loudly to the ground. She turned her head to look at him and the man nodded. "Yes, as I am sure you realize now, you are perhaps one of the unluckiest people ever. My ancestors gave rise to the Nemean Lion. I personally am known as Cleonae."

Juno sighed as she realized just how unlucky this recent turn of events was. According to mythology, a Nemean lion was a creature that possessed unbelievable strength. The skin of a Nemean lion was so durable that nothing could penetrate it, which explained why her daggers had failed completely. Even worse, the mythology indicated a strong preference for taking damsels in distress as hostages to lure unsuspecting warriors. Like most daemon matters, the mythology was not necessarily accurate. Although the skills and talents of daemons had given rise to human mythology, not all of the stories were exactly true. Juno glanced at the strong, impenetrable arm that held her firmly. It unfortunately seemed like the myths about the daemon called the Nemean lion were fairly accurate. Cleonae was certainly one of the strongest men she had ever met.

At the end of the passageway, Cleonae turned into a hallway that led to a flight of spiral stairs. Following the staircase down into the earth, he continued for several floors. As they descended into the bowels of the earth, the moisture and coolness of the air increased. Before long, Juno's eyes had adjusted fully to the darkness. As Cleonae reached for the door handle, she realized exactly where they were. A dungeon.

Realizing that protests would not help her escape, Juno allowed Cleonae to place her inside a cell. Tipping an imaginary hat in her direction, he smiled. "It isn't often that I bring home as lovely of a catch as you," he said. "We'll have to speak more together. For now, I will leave to get Supay or Phoebe."

After he had left the dungeon, Juno waited for his footsteps to fade into the distance before she moved. She paced the dark interior of her cell. There were no cracks in the walls and no windows. Juno looked up. They had not even bothered to put in a light bulb or sink. This was beyond medieval. Groaning, she sank onto a wide bench that lined the back wall of the cell. Somewhere, Apollo was waiting for her to come home. If she did not return, he would think that she had returned to the normal lifestyle that a siren had and forgotten about him. She flinched. Somehow, she would have to beguile her way out of here.

A sound outside of the cell drew her attention. Footsteps were slowly beginning to approach again. Surprisingly, it was just one pair of feet that Juno heard and the steps were light. It must be Phoebe which meant that today was going in an even worse direction than she had expected.

Outside of the door, Phoebe knocked. "Hand the daggers through the door. Cleonae is already prepared to kill you in the event of an escape, but I would prefer not to be stabbed."

Silently, Juno handed the daggers through the window of the door and stepped back. Phoebe swung the door open and gazed around. She looked around the room. Her auburn curls stood out brightly in the dim interior of the dungeon. "Normally, I would apologize that the dungeon is so inhumanely designed. In this case, I think it is appropriate." She leaned against the wall.

Resuming her sitting position on the bench, Juno paused and thought. With Phoebe here, there was no way that she could beguile or seduce her way out of this disaster. She would have to hope that Supay or Cleonae would return at some point. Juno shuddered unintentionally. She was not looking forward to the possibility of seducing Cleonae. He was not unattractive, but he was not really her type. Worse still, if he forgot his strength during sex, she could end up maimed or worse.

Phoebe ran her fingers through her hair and smiled coolly. "This is what you get for ruining my life and Supay's. Do you realize what your meddling has done? I cannot love him completely and have never told him. He knows that I do not love him as much as he loves me, but does not understand why. Your trap worked extremely well. I believe that you deserve to be housed in this exact location."

Juno's eyes lit up. "You know, I could remove the spell from Supay and you. My deal to stay uninvolved would obviously be off, but you would not have the limitations on your feelings in place anymore." She paused. "Of course, I would need to be released from here in trade."

Laughing darkly, Phoebe shook her head. She had learned the hard way to never make a deal with a siren. It would be impossible to ensure that Juno followed through with all parts of the deal. Normally, there was some loophole or hidden intention that made Juno come out on top. For people involved on the other side of the deal, disaster was imminent. "There is no way that I would make another deal with you, siren. Since you seem to have a greater effect on men, I am staffing the dungeon with female guards who will remain on the exterior doors so that they do not hear you. Even Supay will not know of your existence down here."

Wincing, Juno nodded. Perhaps she could one day work to regain Phoebe's trust and escape. Or a weak-willed man would find her here and be easily seduced. "I understand. I was just offering to lift the spell, but you do not have to take the deal."

Phoebe shook her head. "You are right about that. Get rested. Cleonae is going to return to interrogate you," Phoebe saw Juno's eyes brighten and laughed again. "I wouldn't get too excited. Cleonae is more inclined toward hostage taking. He enjoys locking women up here and waiting to fight anyone that tries to save them." She shrugged. "Normally, we would not work with someone like that, but he has his uses." Turning away, Phoebe stepped out of the cell and shut the door.

Behind her, Juno sat up perfectly straight and kept her face emotionless. Once the door slammed shut and Phoebe had left, she sank down to the ground and succumbed to tears. Apollo had no clue where she was and there was no way out.

-To be continued in Book 10-

If you enjoyed this title, I would appreciate your leaving a review of the book. Good reviews encourage an author to write as well as help books to sell. Good reviews can be just a few short sentences describing what you liked about the book without having a spoiler. If you could spend 30 seconds writing a review, I would appreciate it: you can review this title right now at your favorite retailer.

Here is a preview of the **next story** you may enjoy:

The Interrogation - The Daemon Paranormal Romance Chronicles, Book 10

WITHIN THE inner recesses of the cave fortress, Supay was struggling to get everything under control. The impending war with the Roman daemons had everyone on high alert and each Greek daemon had been called to the fortress. Unfortunately, this meant that undesirable creatures like Cleonae had also been brought into the fold. Supay tried to hide his disgust in dealing with these creatures, but found it almost impossible.

After a long day at the fortress, Supay was finally getting a chance to go to bed. Entering the bedroom, he saw Phoebe on the bed. Since Peru, she had been different. Everything had been going perfectly for a while. Once her memories had finally recovered, she had returned from Spain and become the perfect mate for Supay. They had enjoyed living blissfully together with their daughter, Irene, until everything changed one day. At first, Supay thought that he had imagined the change. Little things that Phoebe did seemed different. Over the last few months, he had realized the unfortunate truth: Phoebe had found out about the deal with Juno. Now, she was unable to love him as fully and completely as she had before. Despite this realization, Supay did not do anything to change the situation. He hoped that he was wrong and did not want to make things worse if Phoebe truly did not know.

Hearing Supay enter the room, Phoebe rolled over. "Hey, love. How is everything going? I just put Irene to bed." She smiled and patted the bed invitingly.

Removing his clothes, Supay slid into bed next to her. Although it appeared like most fortresses on the inside, the underground complex became extremely chilly at night. Supay was glad that he could share the bed with Phoebe each night. Rolling toward her, he gently looped her hair behind her ear. "Preparations are underway, although it could always be better. I just wish that we could tell exactly what the Romans are up to right now."

Next to him, Phoebe remained silent. She had avoided telling Supay about Juno. Phoebe knew that Juno had once dated Supay and also knew that Juno was the reason their relationship was starting to fall apart. If Supay knew that Juno was interrogated and tortured in the dungeon, he would never forgive her. Phoebe winced. The torture had not been intentional. She had thought that Cleonae's natural inclination to capture and keep damsels meant that he would protect them. This obviously was not the case. The sadistic Nemean lion daemon had merrily started the interrogation.

Noticing her expression, Supay raised an eyebrow. Something was off, but he did not know what it was. "Phoebe?" he asked.

Distracted from her thoughts for the moment, Phoebe realized that Supay knew she was keeping a secret. She would have to distract him for the moment. "Nothing, Supay, I was just thinking. Wait here." Slipping out of bed, Phoebe went into the closet and found her favorite lingerie. Sliding her body into the black lace, she stepped back and admired her figure. All she needed now was some shoes and possibly lipstick.

After applying a coat of dark red lipstick that matched beautifully with her hair, Phoebe smoothed her hair back into a tight bun. She slipped into tall, black boots. Before leaving the closet, she slipped some elbow-length, black gloves over her hands and arms. She was ready.

Exiting the closet, Phoebe flipped on the music player. Slow-paced, ethereal music flooded the room as she turned on a lone red lamp. Around her, the bedroom had been transformed from a typical sleeping area into a dominatrix's den. Smiling, she walked up to the bed. Supay had remained exactly where she had left him. She motioned for him to spread his arms and legs toward each bed post. Pulling out the bed restraints, Phoebe roped his arms and legs to individual bed posts.

If you enjoyed this sample then look for **The Interrogation - The Daemon Paranormal Romance Chronicles, Book 10**.

Here is a preview of **another story** you may enjoy:

Fury of Lust - The Leather Satchel Romance Series, Book 5

"**VALTINA, I'M** so sorry it took me so long to get back. My superior summoned us all to explain the new protocol. I'm afraid our forces continue to be overwhelmed by the evil armies. Two dozen spirits failed to report back after their assignments this week. Undoubtedly they've been captured by wraiths." Ladaya spoke quickly… time was not a luxury she had, given the current circumstances. She continued, "We can no longer afford to risk sending you out on your own. From now on, you will be accompanied on all of your missions by two protectors… a warrior and an emere. I've assigned Demetri as your warrior… I know you've worked well together in the past. Fatima will be your emere. She will meet you at your destination."

Valtina finally spoke. "Ladaya, what is an emere? I don't think I've ever heard you mention one before."

"I'm sorry, child. Of course you wouldn't know about emeres. The emeres are the purest form of spirits. They left the mortal world when they were infants, so their souls were never tarnished. Fatima and the other emeres have powers far more potent than even my own. And they can move freely between The Afterlife and Earth. They cannot come to Middle World, but Fatima will be able to send you home after your mission, or if you're in imminent danger. I cannot stress this enough, Valtina. You must stay vigilant and be on constant guard against danger."

Valtina was saddened by Ladaya's appearance. Gone was the carefree, wise woman who had guided her on her journey to The Afterlife. Now, Ladaya stood before her in torn robes, her hair undone and wild, and her kind eyes filled with despair. When Valtina had agreed to join the spirit army to fight against the evil forces, she'd imagined that she would receive her final reward after one or two missions. As the weeks went on, however, Valtina realized that she may never reach The Afterlife. Her destiny, it seemed, was to valiantly fight a losing battle.

"Ladaya, what can I expect to run into, besides the tricksters, succubi, and wraiths? I want to be prepared!"

"Valtina, I don't know how many kinds of monsters are now working against us. Morgonda seems to have rallied every creature that's ever been imagined. Our sources tell us that she's breeding them, combining wraith and lampades, demons and nymphs… she's designing her own unique army. I've heard she's even recruited scorned demigods to fight against us."

Valtina gasped. "Demigods? She's turning everything against us, isn't she?"

"She's doing her best to," Ladaya agreed, "but we must not be discouraged. And we must keep fighting. Are you ready for your next assignment?" Valtina responded by nodding. "I'm afraid this one may be your most challenging mission yet. You'll have Demetri and Fatima, of course, but I daresay their powers won't be much help for most of this. They're mainly along for your protection," said Ladaya.

"Ladaya, I know you've insisted on protecting me in the past, but don't Demetri and Fatima have better things to do than shadow me while I fix people's love lives? Surely they could be of more use somewhere else! I can protect myself!" Valtina insisted defiantly. It seemed to her that having two spirit babysitters was overkill. Valtina wanted to end the war as quickly as possible, so she could be reunited with her soul-mate in The Afterlife. If Demetri and Fatima worked their own assignments, they could defeat three evil situations in the time it would take them to defeat one together.

"Valtina, we are *not* arguing about this again," Ladaya answered firmly. "You may not understand your own importance, but the rest of us do. You are the culmination of every type of love that exists. *You* hold within you everything Morgonda and her armies are trying to defeat. We have other loving souls fighting for us, of course, but *you* are the most powerful. There is nothing more important than keeping you safe, and helping you to bring love back to the souls on Earth. *You* are our best chance of ridding the world from evil once and for all, Valtina!"

"Now," Ladaya continued, "your next mission. As I was saying, I'm afraid this will be your most difficult assignment yet. Rachel and Sean were supposed to meet in college and fall in love. They should have been married for six years now, but Morgonda's forces interfered. Rachel was possessed by a fury, and has been leading a dangerous, promiscuous, loveless life ever since. True love is the only power strong enough to expel a fury, so Sean has been well guarded, to ensure that the two never meet. Demons watch him day and night… study them and observe their shift schedule. You'll have to free Sean before you can help Rachel. This is a complicated case, Valtina, and we can't afford for you to become distracted like last time," Ladaya chided. Valtina blushed. During her last mission, she'd wasted nearly 14 hours daydreaming about her lives with her soul-mate. She opened her mouth to offer reassurance, but she was interrupted.

If you enjoyed this sample then look for **Fury of Lust - The Leather Satchel Romance Series, Book 5.**

Other Books by Darla Dunbar

- The Romeo Alpha BBW Paranormal Shifter Romance Series

- Romeo Alpha Blood Lines Romance

- The Alpha Feud BBW Paranormal Shifter Romance Series

- The Alpha Packed BBW Paranormal Shifter Romance Series

- The Mind Talker Paranormal Romance Series

- The Leather Satchel Paranormal Romance Series

Get the latest update on new releases from the author at:

https://darladunbar.com/newsletter/

About the Author - Darla Dunbar

Darla has been interested in paranormal romance since she was a teenager in high school. It was then that she discovered she could fulfill her fantasies through her writing.

Observing people and human behavior in the area of romance has always been one of her favorite pastimes. Combining that with an overactive imagination is a sure fire way of coming up with interesting themes.

Connect with Darla Dunbar

I really appreciate you reading my book! Here are my social media coordinates:

Friend me on Facebook:
https://www.facebook.com/darladunbar/

Follow me on Twitter: https://twitter.com/DarlDunbar

Check me out on Goodreads:
https://www.goodreads.com/author/show/8425857.Darl a_Dunbar

Subscribe to my newsletter:
https://darladunbar.com/newsletter/

Visit my website: https://darladunbar.com/

9 781987 863925